This book is dedicated, in loving memory,
to Edwin Aguilar, and to his pride and joy—
Bodhi, Maya, and Jonathon— who are so loved.

Published by Roaring Brook Press
Roaring Brook Press is a division of Holtzbrinck Publishing Holdings Limited Partnership
120 Broadway, New York, NY 10271 · mackids.com

Library of Congress Cataloging-in-Publication Data is available.
ISBN 978-1-250-80260-6

Our books may be purchased in bulk for promotional, educational, or business use.
Please contact your local bookseller or the Macmillan Corporate and Premium Sales Department
at (800) 221-7945 ext. 5442 or by email at MacmillanSpecialMarkets@macmillan.com.

First edition, 2022
Printed in China by RR Donnelley Asia Printing Solutions Ltd., Dongguan City, Guangdong Province

1 3 5 7 9 10 8 6 4 2

This book was edited by Connie Hsu and Mekisha Telfer.
The designer was Ashley Caswell the art director was Jen Keenan.
The production manager was Allene Cassagnol, and the production editor was Kathy Wielgosz.
The illustrations were created with created with digital magic. The type was set in Merendina.

You're LOVED

Liz Climo

Roaring Brook Press
New York

You're brand new,

and you're perfect.

WAAAAAAA AAAAAAH!

You're demanding,

but you're worth it.

You're small,

and you're fragile.

You're determined,

you're agile.

You're frustrated,

you're frightened,

you're curious

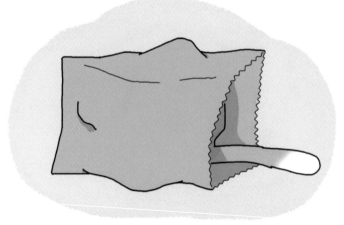

and enlightened.

You're not hungry,

your tummy aches.

You're not tired,

You're smiling, you're giggling.

You're wobbling, you're wiggling.

You're restless, you're loud.

You're smart, and you're proud.

You're taking steps,

you're getting stronger,

you're growing tall

and sleeping longer.

You're building cities, you're painting trees.

You're taking risks and skinning knees.

You're making friends,

you're on your own,

you're bold, you're brave—

oh, how you've grown!

You're older now

but still my baby.

and always will be.